C & T Titles of Related Interest

Family by Pa Chin (Ba Jin), with introduction by Olga Lang, translated by Sidney Shapiro   0-917056-40-X

Secrets: A Collection of Short Stories by Bo Yang, translated by David Deterding

Paper 0-88727-051-4
Cloth 0-88727-037-9

Traditonal Chinese Stories: Themes and Variations, edited by Y. W. Ma and Joseph S. M. Lau

0-88727-071-9

Water Margin by Shih Nai-an, translated by J. H. Jackson   Cloth   0-917056-02-7

Send requests for catalogs of other publications and audio-visual aids in Asian studies to:
Cheng & Tsui Company, 25 West Street, Boston, MA 02111-1268   USA   (Tel: 617-426-6074)

The True Story of Ah Q

The True Story of Ah Q

by Lu Hsun

Translated by
Yang Hsien-yi & Gladys Yang

Cheng & Tsui Company

Library of Congress Catalog Card Number 89-081931

C & T Asian Literature Series

ISBN 0-917056-93-0

Printed in the United States of America

Lu Hsun

Pencil drawing by
Tao Yuan-ching

Contents

CHAPTER I

Introduction

FOR several years now I have been meaning to write the true story of Ah Q. But while wanting to write I was in some trepidation, too, which goes to show that I am not one of those who achieve glory by writing; for an immortal pen has always been required to record the deeds of an immortal man, the man becoming known to posterity through the writing and the writing known to posterity through the man — until finally it is not clear who is making whom known. But in the end, as though possessed by some fiend, I always came back to the idea of writing the story of Ah Q.

And yet no sooner had I taken up my pen than I became conscious of tremendous difficulties in writing this far-from-immortal work. The first was the question of what to call it. Confucius said, "If the name is not correct, the words will not ring true"; and this axiom should be most scrupulously observed. There are many types of biographies: official biographies, autobiographies, unauthorized biographies, legends, supplementary biographies, family histories, sketches . . . but unfortunately none of these suited my purpose. "Official biography?" This account will obviously not be included with those of many eminent people in some authentic history. "Autobiography?" But I am obviously not Ah Q. If I were to call this an "unauthorized biography," then where is his "authenticated biography"? The use of "legend" is impossible, because Ah Q was no legendary figure. "Supplementary biography?" But no president has ever ordered the National Historical Institute to write a "standard life" of Ah Q. It is true that although there are no "lives of gamblers" in authentic English history, the famous author Conan Doyle nevertheless wrote *Rodney Stone*;[1] but while this is permissible for a famous author it is not permissible for such as I. Then there is "family history"; but I do not know whether I belong to the same family as Ah Q or not, nor have his children or grandchildren ever entrusted me with such a task. If I were to use "sketch," it might be objected that Ah Q has no "complete account." In short, this is really a "life," but since I write in vulgar vein using the language of hucksters and pedlars, I dare not presume to give it so high-sounding a title. So from the stock phrase of the novelists, who are not reckoned among the Three Cults and Nine Schools,[2] "Enough of this digression, and back to the *true story*!" I will take the last two words as my title, and if this is reminiscent of the *True Story of Calligraphy*[3] of the ancients, it cannot be helped.

---

[1] In Chinese this novel was called *Supplementary Biographies of the Gamblers*.

[2] The Three Cults were Confucianism, Buddhism and Taoism. The Nine Schools included the Confucian, Taoist, Legalist and Moist schools, as well as others. Novelists, who did not belong to any of these, were considered not quite respectable.

[3] A book by Feng Wu of the Ching dynasty (1644-1911).

The second difficulty confronting me was that a biography of this type should start off something like this: "So-and-so, whose other name was so-and-so, was a native of such-and-such a place"; but I don't really know what Ah Q's surname was. Once, he seemed to be named Chao, but the next day there was some confusion about the matter again. This was after Mr. Chao's son had passed the county examination, and, to the sound of gongs, his success was announced in the village. Ah Q, who had just drunk two bowls of yellow wine, began to prance about declaring that this reflected credit on him too, since he belonged to the same clan as Mr. Chao, and by an exact reckoning was three generations senior to the successful candidate. At the time several bystanders even began to stand slightly in awe of Ah Q. But the next day the bailiff summoned him to Mr. Chao's house. When the old gentleman set eyes on him his face turned crimson with fury and he roared:

"Ah Q, you miserable wretch! Did you say I belonged to the same clan as you?"

Ah Q made no reply.

The more he looked at him the angrier Mr. Chao became, and advancing menacingly a few steps he said, "How dare you talk such nonsense! How could I have such a relative as you? Is your surname Chao?"

Ah Q made no reply, and was planning a retreat, when Mr. Chao darted forward and gave him a slap on the face.

"How could *you* be named Chao! — Do you think you are worthy of the name Chao?"

Ah Q made no attempt to defend his right to the name Chao, but rubbing his left cheek went out with the bailiff. Once outside, he had to listen to another torrent of abuse

3

from the bailiff, and thank him to the tune of two hundred cash. All who heard this said Ah Q was a great fool to ask for a beating like that. Even if his surname *were* Chao — which wasn't likely — he should have known better than to boast like that when there was a Mr. Chao living in the village. After this no further mention was made of Ah Q's ancestry, so that I still don't know what his surname really was.

The third difficulty I encountered in writing this work was that I don't know how Ah Q's personal name should be written either. During his lifetime everybody called him Ah Quei, but after his death not a soul mentioned Ah Quei again; for he was obviously not one of those whose name is "preserved on bamboo tablets and silk."[1] If there is any question of preserving his name, this essay must be the first attempt at doing so. Hence I am confronted with this difficulty at the outset. I have given the question careful thought: Ah Quei — would that be the "Quei" meaning cassia or the "Quei" meaning nobility? If his other name had been Moon Pavilion, or if he had celebrated his birthday in the month of the Moon Festival, then it would certainly be the "Quei" for cassia.[2] But since he had no other name — or if he had, no one knew it — and since he never sent out invitations on his birthday to secure complimentary verses, it would be arbitrary to write Ah Quei (cassia). Again, if he had had an

---

[1] A phrase first used in the third century B.C. Bamboo and silk were writing material in ancient China.

[2] The cassia blooms in the month of the Moon Festival. Also, according to Chinese folklore, it is believed that the shadow on the moon is a cassia tree.

elder or younger brother called Ah Fu (prosperity), then he would certainly be called Ah Quei (nobility). But he was all on his own: thus there is no justification for writing Ah Quei (nobility). All the other, unusual characters with the sound Quei are even less suitable. I once put this question to Mr. Chao's son, the successful county candidate, but even such a learned man as he was baffled by it. According to him, however, the reason why this name could not be traced was that Chen Tu-hsiu[1] had brought out the magazine *New Youth,* advocating the use of the Western alphabet, so that the national culture was going to the dogs. As a last resort, I asked someone from my district to go and look up the legal documents recording Ah Q's case, but after eight months he sent me a letter saying that there was no name anything like Ah Quei in those records. Although uncertain whether this was the truth or whether my friend had simply done nothing, after failing to trace the name this way I could think of no other means of finding it. Since I am afraid the new system of phonetics has not yet come into common use, there is nothing for it but to use the Western alphabet, writing the name according to the English spelling as Ah Quei and abbreviating it to Ah Q. This approximates to blindly following the *New Youth* magazine, and I am thoroughly ashamed of myself; but since even such a learned man as Mr. Chao's son could not solve my problem, what else can I do?

My fourth difficulty was with Ah Q's place of origin. If his surname were Chao, then according to the old custom

---

[1] 1880-1942. A professor of Peking University at this time, he edited the monthly *New Youth.* Later he became a renegade from the Chinese Communist Party.

which still prevails of classifying people by their districts, one might look up the commentary in *The Hundred Surnames*[1] and find "A native of Tienshui in Kansu Province." But unfortunately this surname is open to question, with the result that Ah Q's place of origin must also remain uncertain. Although he lived for the most part in Weichuang, he often stayed in other places, so that it would be wrong to call him a native of Weichuang. It would, in fact, amount to a distortion of history.

The only thing that consoles me is the fact that the character "Ah" is absolutely correct. This is definitely not the result of false analogy, and is well able to stand the test of scholarly criticism. As for the other problems, it is not for such unlearned people as myself to solve them, and I can only hope that disciples of Dr. Hu Shih, who has such "a passion for history and antiquities,"[2] may be able in future to throw new light on them. I am afraid, however, that by that time my *True Story of Ah Q* will have long since passed into oblivion.

The foregoing may be considered as an introduction.

---

[1] A school primer, in which the surnames were written into verse.

[2] This phrase was often used in self-praise by Hu Shih, the well-known reactionary politician and writer.

CHAPTER 2

A Brief Account of Ah Q's Victories

In addition to the uncertainty regarding Ah Q's surname, personal name, and place of origin, there is even some uncertainty regarding his "background." This is because the people of Weichuang only made use of his services or treated him as a laughing-stock, without ever paying the slightest attention to his "background." Ah Q himself remained silent on this subject, except that when quarrelling with someone he might glance at him and say, "We used to be much better off than you! Who do you think you are anyway?"

Ah Q had no family but lived in the Tutelary God's Temple at Weichuang. He had no regular work either, simply doing odd jobs for others: were there wheat to be cut he would cut it, were there rice to be ground he would grind it, were there a boat to be punted he would punt it. If the work lasted for a considerable period he might stay in the house of his temporary employer, but as soon as it was finished he would leave. Thus whenever people had work

7

to be done they would remember Ah Q, but what they remembered was his service and not his "background"; and by the time the job was done even Ah Q himself was forgotten, to say nothing of his "background." Once indeed an old man remarked, "What a good worker Ah Q is!" At that time Ah Q, stripped to the waist, listless and lean, was standing before him, and other people did not know whether the remark was meant seriously or derisively, but Ah Q was overjoyed.

Ah Q, again, had a very high opinion of himself. He looked down on all the inhabitants of Weichuang, thinking even the two young "scholars" not worth a smile, though most young scholars were likely to pass the official examinations. Mr. Chao and Mr. Chien were held in great respect by the villagers, for in addition to being rich they were both the fathers of young scholars. Ah Q alone showed them no exceptional deference, thinking to himself, "My sons may be much greater!"

Moreover, after Ah Q had been to town several times, he naturally became even more conceited, although at the same time he had the greatest contempt for townspeople. For instance, a bench made of a wooden plank three feet by three inches the Weichuang villagers called a "long bench." Ah Q called it a "long bench" too; but the townspeople called it a "straight bench," and he thought, "This is wrong. How ridiculous!" Again, when they fried large-headed fish in oil the Weichuang villagers all added shallot leaves sliced half an inch long, whereas the townspeople added finely shredded shallots, and he thought, "This is wrong too. How

ridiculous!" But the Weichuang villagers were really igno-
rant rustics who had never seen fish fried in town!

Ah Q who "used to be much better off," who was a man
of the world and "a good worker," would have been almost
the perfect man had it not been for a few unfortunate physical blemishes. The most annoying were some places on
his scalp where in the past, at some uncertain date, shiny
ringworm scars had appeared. Although these were on his
own head, apparently Ah Q did not consider them as alto-
gether honourable, for he refrained from using the word
"ringworm" or any words that sounded anything like it.
Later he improved on this, making "bright" and "light" for-
bidden words, while later still even "lamp" and "candle"
were taboo. Whenever this taboo was disregarded, whether
intentionally or not, Ah Q would fly into a rage, his ringworm scars turning scarlet. He would look over the offender,
and if it were someone weak in repartee he would curse
him, while if it were a poor fighter he would hit him. Yet,
curiously enough, it was usually Ah Q who was worsted
in these encounters, until finally he adopted new tactics, con-
tenting himself in general with a furious glare. *new tactics to survive*

It so happened, however, that after Ah Q had taken to
using this furious glare, the idlers in Weichuang grew even
more fond of making jokes at his expense. As soon as they
saw him they would pretend to give a start, and say:

"Look! It's lighting up."

Ah Q would rise to the bait as usual, and glare furiously.

"So there is a paraffin lamp here," they would continue,
not in the least intimidated.

9

Ah Q could do nothing but rack his brains for some re-tort: "You don't even deserve. . . ." At this juncture it seemed as if the scars on his scalp were noble and honour-able, not just ordinary ringworm scars. However, as we said above, Ah Q was a man of the world: he knew at once that he had nearly broken the "taboo" and refrained from saying any more.

If the idlers were still not satisfied, but continued to bait him, they would in the end come to blows. Then only after Ah Q had, to all appearances, been defeated, had his brown-ish pigtail pulled and his head bumped against the wall four or five times, would the idlers walk away, satisfied at having won. Ah Q would stand there for a second, thinking to himself, "It is as if I were beaten by my son. What is the world coming to nowadays. . . ." Thereupon he too would walk away, satisfied at having won.

Whatever Ah Q thought he was sure to tell people later; thus almost all who made fun of Ah Q knew that he had this means of winning a psychological victory. So after this anyone who pulled or twisted his brown pigtail would fore-stall him by saying: "Ah Q, this is not a son beating his father, it is a man beating a beast. Let's hear you say it: A man beating a beast!"

Then Ah Q, clutching at the root of his pigtail, his head on one side, would say: "Beating an insect — how about that? I am an insect — now will you let me go?"

But although he was an insect the idlers would not let him go until they had knocked his head five or six times against something nearby, according to their custom, after which they would walk away satisfied that they had won, confident that this time Ah Q was done for. In less than ten seconds, however, Ah Q would walk away also satisfied that he had won, thinking that he was the "foremost self-belittler," and that after subtracting "self-belittler" what remained was "foremost." Was not the highest successful candidate in the official examination also the "foremost"? "And who do you think you are anyway?"

After employing such cunning devices to get even with his enemies, Ah Q would make his way cheerfully to the wineshop to drink a few bowls of wine, joke with the others again, quarrel with them again, come off victorious again, and return cheerfully to the Tutelary God's Temple, there to fall asleep as soon as his head touched the pillow. If he had money he would gamble. A group of men would squat on the ground, Ah Q sandwiched in their midst, his face streaming with perspiration; and his voice would shout the loudest: "Four hundred on the Green Dragon!"

"Hey — open there!" the stakeholder, his face streaming with perspiration too, would open the box and chant: "Heavenly Gate! . . . Nothing for the Corner! . . . No stakes on the Popularity Passage! Pass over Ah Q's coppers!"

"The Passage — one hundred — one hundred and fifty."

To the tune of this chanting, Ah Q's money would gradually vanish into the pockets of other perspiring people. Finally he would be forced to squeeze his way out of the crowd and watch from the back, taking a vicarious interest in the game until it broke up, when he would return reluctantly to the Tutelary God's Temple. The next day he would go to work with swollen eyes.

However, the truth of the proverb "misfortune may be a blessing in disguise" was shown when Ah Q was unfortunate enough to win and almost suffered defeat in the end.

This was the evening of the Festival of the Gods in Weichuang. According to custom there was a play; and close to the stage, also according to custom, were numerous gambling tables. The drums and gongs of the play sounded about three miles away to Ah Q who had ears only for the stakeholder's chant. He staked successfully again and again, his coppers turning into silver coins, his silver coins into dollars, and his dollars mounting up. In his excitement he cried out, "Two dollars on Heavenly Gate!"

He never knew who started the fight, nor for what reason. Curses, blows and footsteps formed a confused medley of sound in his head, and by the time he clambered to his feet the gambling tables had vanished and so had the gamblers. Several parts of his body seemed to be aching as if he had been kicked and knocked about, while a number of people were looking at him in astonishment. Feeling as if there were something amiss, he walked back to the Tutelary God's Temple, and by the time he regained his composure he realized that his pile of dollars had disappeared. Since most of the people who ran gambling tables at the Festival were not natives of Weichuang, where could he look for the culprits?

So white and glittering a pile of silver! It had all been his . . . but now it had disappeared. Even to consider it tantamount to being robbed by his son did not comfort him. To consider himself as an insect did not comfort him either. This time he really tasted something of the bitterness of defeat.

But presently he changed defeat into victory. Raising his right hand he slapped his own face hard twice, so that it tingled with pain. After this slapping his heart felt lighter, for it seemed as if the one who had given the slap was himself, the one slapped some other self, and soon it was just as if he had beaten someone else — in spite of the fact that his face was still tingling. He lay down satisfied that he had gained the victory.

Soon he was asleep.

CHAPTER 3

A Further Account of Ah Q's Victories

ALTHOUGH Ah Q was always gaining victories, it was only after he was favoured with a slap on the face by Mr. Chao that he became famous.

After paying the bailiff two hundred cash he lay down angrily. Later he said to himself, "What is the world coming to nowadays, with sons beating their parents. . . ." Then the thought of the prestige of Mr. Chao, who was now his son, gradually raised his spirits, and he got up and went to the wineshop singing *The Young Widow at Her Husband's Grave*. At that time he did feel that Mr. Chao was a cut above most people.

After this incident, strange to relate, it was true that everybody seemed to pay him unusual respect. He probably attributed this to the fact that he was Mr. Chao's father, but actually such was not the case. In Weichuang, as a rule, if the seventh child hit the eighth child or Li So-and-so hit Chang So-and-so, it was not taken seriously. A beating had to be connected with some important personage like Mr.

Chao before the villagers thought it worth talking about. But once they thought it worth talking about, since the beater was famous, the one beaten enjoyed some of his reflected fame. As for the fault being Ah Q's, that was naturally taken for granted, the reason being that Mr. Chao could not possibly be wrong. But if Ah Q were wrong, why did everybody seem to treat him with unusual respect? This is difficult to explain. We may put forward the hypothesis that it was because Ah Q had said he belonged to the same family as Mr. Chao; thus, although he had been beaten, people were still afraid there might be some truth in what he said and therefore thought it safer to treat him more respectfully. Or, alternatively, it may have been like the case of the sacrificial beef in the Confucian temple: although the beef was in the same category as the sacrificial pork and mutton, being of animal origin just as they were, later Confucians did not dare touch it since the sage had enjoyed it.

After this Ah Q prospered for several years.

One spring, when he was walking along in a state of happy intoxication, he saw Whiskers Wang sitting stripped to the waist in the sunlight at the foot of a wall, catching lice; and at this sight his own body began to itch. Since Whiskers Wang was scabby and bewhiskered, everybody called him "Ringworm Whiskers Wang." Although Ah Q omitted the word "Ringworm," he had the greatest contempt for the man. Ah Q felt that while scabs were nothing to take exception to, such hairy cheeks were really too outlandish, and could excite nothing but scorn. So Ah Q sat down by his side. If it had been any other idler, Ah Q would never have dared sit down so casually; but what had he to fear by the side of Whiskers Wang? To tell the truth, the fact that he was willing to sit down was an honour for Wang.

Ah Q took off his tattered lined jacket, and turned it inside out; but either because he had washed it recently or because he was too clumsy, a long search yielded only three or four lice. He saw that Whiskers Wang, on the other hand, was catching first one and then another in swift succession, cracking them in his teeth with a popping sound.

Ah Q felt first disappointed, then resentful: the despicable Whiskers Wang could catch so many while he himself had caught so few — what a great loss of face! He longed to catch one or two big ones, but there were none, and it was only with considerable difficulty that he managed to catch a middle-sized one, which he thrust fiercely into his mouth and bit savagely; but it only gave a small sputtering sound, again inferior to the noise Whiskers Wang was making.

All Ah Q's scars turned scarlet. Flinging his jacket on the ground, he spat and said, "Hairy worm!"

"Mangy dog, who are you calling names?" Whiskers Wang looked up contemptuously.

Although the relative respect accorded him in recent years had increased Ah Q's pride, when confronted by loafers who were accustomed to fighting he remained rather timid. On this occasion, however, he was feeling exceptionally pugnacious. How dare a hairy-cheeked creature like this insult him?

"Anyone who the name fits," said Ah Q standing up, his hands on his hips.

"Are your bones itching?" demanded Whiskers Wang, standing up too and putting on his coat.

Thinking that Wang meant to run away, Ah Q stepped forward raising his fist to punch him. But before his fist came down, Whiskers Wang had already seized him and given him a tug which sent him staggering. Then Whiskers Wang seized Ah Q's pigtail and started dragging him towards the wall to knock his head in the time-honoured manner.

" 'A gentleman uses his tongue but not his hands!' " protested Ah Q, his head on one side.

Apparently Whiskers Wang was no gentleman, for without paying the slightest attention to what Ah Q said he knocked his head against the wall five times in succession, and gave him a great shove which sent him staggering two yards away. Only then did Whiskers Wang walk away satisfied.

As far as Ah Q could remember, this was the first humiliation of his life, because he had always scoffed at Whiskers Wang on account of his ugly bewhiskered cheeks, but had never been scoffed at, much less beaten by him. And now, contrary to all expectations, Whiskers Wang had beaten him. Perhaps what they said in the market-place was really true: "The Emperor has abolished the official examinations, so that scholars who have passed them are no longer in demand." As a result of this the Chao family must have lost prestige. Was it a result of this, too, that people were treating him contemptuously?

Ah Q stood there irresolutely.

From the distance approached another of Ah Q's enemies. This was Mr. Chien's eldest son whom Ah Q also despised. After studying in a foreign school in the city, it seemed he had gone to Japan. When he came home half a year later his legs were straight[1] and his pigtail had disappeared. His

---

[1] When the Chinese of those days saw foreigners walking with big strides — unlike the usual Chinese gait — they imagined that foreigners had no joints at the knees.

mother cried bitterly a dozen times, and his wife tried three times to jump into the well. Later his mother told everyone, "His pigtail was cut off by some scoundrel when he was drunk. He would have been able to be an official, but now he will have to wait until it has grown again before he thinks of that." Ah Q did not, however, believe this, and insisted on calling him "Imitation Foreign Devil" and "Traitor in Foreign Pay." As soon as Ah Q saw him he would start cursing under his breath.

What Ah Q despised and detested most in him was his false pigtail. When it came to having a false pigtail, a man could scarcely be considered human; and the fact that his wife had not attempted to jump into the well a fourth time showed that she was not a good woman either.

Now this "Imitation Foreign Devil" was approaching.

"Baldhead — Ass — " In the past Ah Q had cursed under his breath only, inaudibly; but today, because he was in a bad temper and wanted to work off his feelings, the words slipped out involuntarily.

Unfortunately this "baldhead" was carrying a shiny, brown stick which Ah Q called a "staff carried by the mourner." With great strides he bore down on Ah Q who, guessing at once that a beating was impending, hastily braced himself to wait with a stiffened back. Sure enough, there was a resounding thwack which seemed to have alighted on his head.

"I meant him!" explained Ah Q, pointing to a nearby child.

Thwack! Thwack! Thwack!

As far as Ah Q could remember, this was the second humiliation of his life. Fortunately after the thwacking stopped it seemed to him that the matter was closed, and he even felt somewhat relieved. Moreover, the precious "ability to forget" handed down by his ancestors stood him in good stead. He walked slowly away and by the time he approached the wineshop door he felt quite happy again.

Just then, however, a small nun from the Convent of Quiet Self-improvement came walking towards him. The sight of a nun always made Ah Q swear; how much more so, then, after these humiliations? When he recalled what had happened, all his anger revived.

"So all my bad luck today was because I had to see you!" he thought to himself.

He went up to her and spat noisily. "Ugh! . . . Pah!"

The small nun paid not the least attention, but walked on with lowered head. Ah Q went up to her and shot out a hand to rub her newly shaved scalp, then laughing stupidly said, "Baldhead! Go back quickly, your monk is waiting for you. . . ."

"Who are you pawing? . . ." demanded the nun, blushing crimson as she began to hurry away.

The men in the wineshop roared with laughter. Seeing that his feat was admired, Ah Q began to feel elated.

"If the monk paws you, why can't I?" said he, pinching her cheek.

Again the men in the wineshop roared with laughter. Ah Q felt even more pleased, and in order to satisfy those who were expressing approval, he pinched her hard again before letting her go.

During this encounter he had already forgotten Whiskers Wang and the Imitation Foreign Devil, as if all the day's bad luck had been avenged. And, strange to relate, even more relaxed than after the beating, he felt light and buoyant as if ready to float into the air.

"Ah Q, may you die sonless!" sounded the little nun's voice tearfully in the distance.

Ah Q roared with delighted laughter.

The men in the wineshop roared too, with only slightly less satisfaction.

CHAPTER 4

The Tragedy of Love

THERE are said to be some victors who take no pleasure in a victory unless their opponents are as fierce as tigers or eagles: if their adversaries are as timid as sheep or chickens they find their triumph empty. There are other victors who, having carried all before them, with the enemy slain or surrendered, cowering in utter subjection, realize that now no foe, rival, or friend is left — they have only themselves, supreme, solitary, desolate, and forlorn. Then they find their triumph a tragedy. But our hero was not so spineless. He was always exultant. This may be a proof of the moral supremacy of China over the rest of the world.

Look at Ah Q, light and elated, as if about to fly!

This victory was not without strange consequences, though. For quite a time he seemed to be flying, and he flew into the Tutelary God's Temple, where he would normally have snored as soon as he lay down. This evening, however, he found it very difficult to close his eyes, for he felt as if there were something the matter with his thumb and first finger, which seemed to be smoother than usual. It is impossible to say whether something soft and smooth on the little nun's face had stuck to his fingers, or whether his fingers had been rubbed smooth against her cheek.

"Ah Q, may you die sonless!"

These words sounded again in Ah Q's ears, and he thought, "Quite right, I should take a wife; for if a man dies sonless he has no one to sacrifice a bowl of rice to his spirit . . . I ought to have a wife." As the saying goes, "There are three forms of unfilial conduct, of which the worst is to have no descendants,"[1] and it is one of the tragedies of life that "spirits without descendants go hungry."[2] Thus his view was absolutely in accordance with the teachings of the saints and sages, and it is indeed a pity that later he should have run amok.

"Woman, woman! . . ." he thought.

". . . The monk paws. . . . Woman, woman! . . . Woman!" he thought again.

We shall never know when Ah Q finally fell asleep that evening. After this, however, he probably always found his fingers rather soft and smooth, and always remained a little light-headed. "Woman . . ." he kept thinking.

From this we can see that woman is a menace to mankind.

The majority of Chinese men could become saints and sages, were it not for the unfortunate fact that they are ruined by women. The Shang dynasty was destroyed by Ta Chi, the Chou dynasty was undermined by Pao Szu; as for the Chin dynasty, although there is no historical evidence to that effect, if we assume that it fell on account of some

---

[1] A quotation from Mencius (372-289 B.C.).

[2] A quotation from the old classic *Tso Chuan*.

22

woman we shall probably not be far wrong. And it is a fact that Tung Cho's death was caused by Tiao Chan.[1]

Ah Q, too, was a man of strict morals to begin with. Although we do not know whether he was guided by some good teacher, he had always shown himself most scrupulous in observing "strict segregation of the sexes," and was righteous enough to denounce such heretics as the little nun and the Imitation Foreign Devil. His view was, "All nuns must carry on in secret with monks. If a woman walks alone on the street, she must want to seduce bad men. When a man and a woman talk together, it must be to arrange to meet." In order to correct such people, he would glare furiously, pass loud, cutting remarks, or, if the place were deserted, throw a small stone from behind.

Who could tell that close on thirty, when a man should "stand firm,"[2] he would lose his head like this over a little nun? Such light-headedness, according to the classical canons, is most reprehensible; thus women certainly are hateful creatures. For if the little nun's face had not been soft and smooth, Ah Q would not have been bewitched by her; nor would this have happened if the little nun's face had been covered by a cloth. Five or six years before, when watching an open-air opera, he had pinched the leg of a woman in the

---

[1] Ta Chi, of the twelfth century B.C., was the concubine of the last king of the Shang dynasty. Pao Szu, of the eighth century B.C., was the concubine of the last king of the Western Chou dynasty. Tiao Chan was the concubine of Tung Cho, a powerful minister of the third century A.D.

[2] Confucius said that at thirty he "stood firm." The phrase was later used to indicate that a man was thirty years old.

audience; but because it was separated from him by the cloth of her trousers he had not had this light-headed feeling afterwards. The little nun had not covered her face, however, and this is another proof of the odiousness of the heretic.

"Woman . . ." thought Ah Q.

He kept a close watch on those women who he believed must "want to seduce bad men," but they did not smile at him. He listened very carefully to those women who talked to him, but not one of them mentioned anything relevant to a secret rendezvous. Ah! This was simply another example of the odiousness of women: they all assumed a false modesty.

One day when Ah Q was grinding rice in Mr. Chao's house, he sat down in the kitchen after supper to smoke a pipe. If it had been anyone else's house, he could have gone home after supper, but they dined early in the Chao family. Although it was the rule that you must not light a lamp, but go to bed after eating, there were occasional exceptions to the rule. Before Mr. Chao's son passed the county examination he was allowed to light a lamp to study the examination essays, and when Ah Q went to do odd jobs he was allowed to light a lamp to grind rice. Because of this latter exception to the rule, Ah Q still sat in the kitchen smoking before going on with his work.

When Amah Wu, the only maidservant in the Chao household, had finished washing the dishes, she sat down on the long bench too and started chatting to Ah Q:

"Our mistress hasn't eaten anything for two days, because the master wants to get a concubine. . . ."

"Woman . . . Amah Wu . . . this little widow," thought Ah Q.

"Our young mistress is going to have a baby in the eighth moon. . . ."

"Woman . . ." thought Ah Q.

He put down his pipe and stood up.

"Our young mistress — " Amah Wu chattered on.

"Sleep with me!" Ah Q suddenly rushed forward and threw himself at her feet.

There was a moment of absolute silence.

"Ai ya!" Dumbfounded for an instant, Amah Wu suddenly began to tremble, then rushed out shrieking and could soon be heard sobbing.

Ah Q kneeling opposite the wall was dumbfounded too. He grasped the empty bench with both hands and stood up slowly, dimly aware that something was wrong. In fact, by this time he was in rather a nervous state himself. In a flurry, he stuck his pipe into his belt and decided to go back to the rice. But — bang! — a heavy blow landed on his head, and he spun round to see the successful county candidate standing before him brandishing a big bamboo pole.

"How dare you . . . you. . . ."

The big bamboo pole came down across Ah Q's shoulders. When he put up both hands to protect his head, the blow landed on his knuckles, causing him considerable pain. As he escaped through the kitchen door it seemed as if his back also received a blow.

"Turtle's egg!" shouted the successful candidate, cursing him in mandarin from behind.

Ah Q fled to the hulling-floor where he stood alone, still feeling a pain in his knuckles and still remembering that "turtle's egg" because it was an expression never used by the Weichuang villagers, but only by the rich who had seen something of official life. This made him more frightened, and left an exceptionally deep impression on his mind. By now, however, all thought of "Woman . . ." had flown. After this cursing and beating it seemed as if something were done with, and quite light-heartedly he began to grind rice again. After grinding for some time he felt hot, and stopped to take off his shirt.

While he was taking off his shirt he heard an uproar outside, and since Ah Q always liked to join in any excitement that was going, he went out in search of the sound. He traced it gradually right into Mr. Chao's inner courtyard. Although it was dusk he could see many people there: all the Chao family including the mistress who had not eaten for two days. In addition, their neighbour Mrs. Tsou was there, as well as their relatives Chao Pai-yen and Chao Szu-chen.

The young mistress was leading Amah Wu out of the servants' quarters, saying as she did so:

"Come outside . . . don't stay brooding in your own room."

"Everybody knows you are a good woman," put in Mrs. Tsou from the side. "You mustn't think of committing suicide."

Amah Wu merely wailed, muttering something inaudible.

"This is interesting," thought Ah Q. "What mischief can this little widow be up to?" Wanting to find out, he was approaching Chao Szu-chen when suddenly he caught sight of Mr. Chao's eldest son rushing towards him with, what was worse, the big bamboo pole in his hand. The sight of this big bamboo pole reminded him that he had been beaten by it, and he realized that apparently he was connected in some way with this scene of excitement. He turned and ran, hoping to escape to the hulling-floor, not foreseeing that the bamboo pole would cut off his retreat; thereupon he turned and ran in the other direction, leaving without further ado by the back door. In a short time he was back in the Tutelary God's Temple.

After Ah Q had sat down for a time, his skin began to form goose pimples and he felt cold, because although it was spring the nights were still quite frosty and not suited to bare backs. He remembered that he had left his shirt in the Chaos' house, but he was afraid if he went to fetch it he might get another taste of the successful candidate's bamboo pole.

Then the bailiff came in.

"Curse you, Ah Q!" said the bailiff. "So you can't even keep your hands off the Chao family servants, you rebel! You've made me lose my sleep, curse you! . . ."

Under this torrent of abuse Ah Q naturally had nothing to say. Finally, since it was night-time, Ah Q had to pay double and give the bailiff four hundred cash. Because he happened to have no ready money by him, he gave his felt hat as security, and agreed to the following five terms:

1. The next morning Ah Q must take a pair of red candles, weighing one pound, and a bundle of incense sticks to the Chao family to atone for his misdeeds.
2. Ah Q must pay for the Taoist priests whom the Chao family had called to exorcize evil spirits.
3. Ah Q must never again set foot in the Chao household.
4. If anything unfortunate should happen to Amah Wu, Ah Q must be held responsible.
5. Ah Q must not go back for his wages or shirt.

Ah Q naturally agreed to everything, but unfortunately he had no ready money. Luckily it was already spring, so it was possible to do without his padded quilt which he pawned for two thousand cash to comply with the terms stipulated. After kowtowing with bare back he still had a few cash left, but instead of using these to redeem his felt hat from the bailiff, he spent them all on drink.

Actually, the Chao family burned neither the incense nor the candles, because these could be used when the mistress worshipped Buddha and were put aside for that purpose. Most of the ragged shirt was made into diapers for the baby which was born to the young mistress in the eighth moon, while the tattered remainder was used by Amah Wu to make shoe soles.

CHAPTER 5

The Problem of Livelihood

AFTER Ah Q had kowtowed and complied with the Chao family's terms, he went back as usual to the Tutelary God's Temple. The sun had gone down, and he began to feel that something was wrong. Careful thought led him to the conclusion that this was probably because his back was bare. Remembering that he still had a ragged lined jacket, he put it on and lay down, and when he opened his eyes again the sun was already shining on the top of the west wall. He sat up, saying, "Curse it. . . ."

After getting up he loafed about the streets as usual, until he began to feel that something else was wrong, though this was not to be compared to the physical discomfort of a bare back. Apparently, from that day onwards all the women in Weichuang became shy of Ah Q: whenever they saw him coming they took refuge indoors. In fact, even Mrs. Tsou who was nearly fifty years old retreated in confusion with the rest, calling her eleven-year-old daughter to go inside. This struck Ah Q as very strange. "The bitches!" he thought. "They have suddenly become as coy as young ladies. . . ."

A good many days later, however, he felt even more strongly that something was wrong. First, the wineshop refused him credit; secondly, the old man in charge of the Tutelary God's Temple made some uncalled-for remarks, as if he wanted Ah Q to leave; and thirdly, for many days — how many exactly he could not remember — not a soul had come to hire him. To be refused credit in the wineshop he could put up with; if the old man kept urging him to leave, Ah Q could just ignore his complaints; but when no one came to hire him he had to go hungry; and this was really a "cursed" state to be in.

When Ah Q could stand it no longer he went to his regular employers' houses to find out what was the matter — it was only Mr. Chao's threshold that he was not allowed to cross. But he met with a very strange reception. The one to appear was always a man, who looked thoroughly annoyed and waved Ah Q away as if he were a beggar, saying:

"There is nothing, nothing at all! Go away!"

Ah Q found it more and more extraordinary. "These people always needed help in the past," he thought. "They can't suddenly have nothing to be done. This looks fishy." After making careful enquiries he found out that when they had any odd jobs they all called in Young D. Now this Young D was a lean and weakly pauper, even lower in Ah Q's eyes than Whiskers Wang. Who could have thought that this low fellow would steal his living from him? So this time Ah Q's indignation was greater than usual, and going on his way, fuming, he suddenly raised his arm and sang: *"I'll thrash you with a steel mace. . . ."*[1]

---

[1] A line from *The Battle of Dragon and Tiger,* an opera popular in Shaohsing. It told how Chao Kuang-yin, the first emperor of the Sung dynasty, fought with another general.

A few days later he did indeed meet Young D in front of Mr. Chien's house. "When two foes meet, their eyes flash fire." As Ah Q went up to him, Young D stood still.

"Stupid ass!" hissed Ah Q, glaring furiously and foaming at the mouth.

"I'm an insect — will that do? . . ." asked Young D.

Such modesty only made Ah Q angrier than ever, but since he had no steel mace in his hand all he could do was to rush forward with outstretched hand to seize Young D's pigtail. Young D, while protecting his pigtail with one hand, tried to seize Ah Q's with the other, whereupon Ah Q also used one free hand to protect his own pigtail. In the past Ah Q had never considered Young D worth taking seriously, but since he had recently suffered from hunger himself he was now as thin and weak as his opponent, so that they presented a spectacle of evenly matched antagonists. Four hands clutched at two heads, both men bending at the waist, cast a blue, rainbow-shaped shadow on the Chien family's white wall for over half an hour.

"All right! All right!" exclaimed some of the onlookers, probably trying to make peace.

"Good, good!" exclaimed others, but whether to make peace, applaud the fighters or incite them on to further efforts, is not certain.

The two combatants turned deaf ears to them all, however. If Ah Q advanced three paces, Young D would recoil three paces, and so they would stand. If Young D advanced three paces, Ah Q would recoil three paces, and so they would stand again. After about half an hour — Weichuang had few striking clocks, so it is difficult to tell the time; it may have been twenty minutes — when steam was rising from their heads and sweat pouring down their cheeks, Ah Q let fall his hands, and in the same second Young D's hands fell too. They straightened up simultaneously and stepped back simultaneously, pushing their way out through the crowd.

"You'll be hearing from me again, curse you! . . ." said Ah Q over his shoulder.

"Curse you! You'll be hearing from me again . . ." echoed Young D, also over his shoulder.

This epic struggle had apparently ended neither in victory nor defeat, and it is not known whether the spectators were satisfied or not, for none of them expressed any opinion. But still not a soul came to hire Ah Q.

One warm day, when a balmy breeze seemed to give some foretaste of summer, Ah Q actually felt cold; but he could put up with this — his greatest worry was an empty stomach. His cotton quilt, felt hat and shirt had long since disappeared, and after that he had sold his padded jacket. Now nothing was left but his trousers, and these of course he could not take off. He had a ragged lined jacket, it is true; but this was certainly worthless, unless he gave it away to be made into shoe soles. He had long hoped to pick up a sum of money on the road, but hitherto he had not been successful; he had also hoped he might suddenly discover a sum of money in his tumble-down room, and had looked wildly all through it, but the room was quite, quite empty. Thereupon he made up his mind to go out in search of food.

As he walked along the road "in search of food" he saw the familiar wineshop and the familiar steamed bread, but he passed them by without pausing for a second, without even hankering after them. It was not these he was looking for, although what exactly he was looking for he did not know himself.

Since Weichuang was not a big place, he soon left it behind. Most of the country outside the village consisted of paddy fields, green as far as the eye could see with the tender shoots of young rice, dotted here and there with round, black, moving objects, which were peasants cultivating the fields. But blind to the delights of country life, Ah Q simply went on his way, for he knew instinctively that this was far removed from his "search for food." Finally, however, he came to the walls of the Convent of Quiet Self-improvement.

The convent too was surrounded by paddy fields, its white walls standing out sharply in the fresh green, and inside the low earthen wall at the back was a vegetable garden. Ah Q hesitated for a time, looking around him. Since there was no one in sight he scrambled on to the low wall, holding on to some milkwort. The mud wall started crumbling, and Ah Q shook with fear; however, by clutching at the branch of a mulberry tree he managed to jump over it. Within was a wild profusion of vegetation, but no sign of yellow wine, steamed bread, or anything edible. A clump of bamboos, with many young shoots, grew by the west wall but unfortunately these shoots were not cooked. There was also rape which had long since gone to seed; the mustard was already about to flower, and the small cabbages looked very tough.

Ah Q felt as resentful as a scholar who has failed in the examinations. As he walked slowly towards the gate of the garden he gave a start of joy, for there before him what did he see but a patch of turnips! He knelt down and began pulling, when suddenly a round head appeared from behind the gate, only to be withdrawn again at once. This was no other than the little nun. Now though Ah Q had always had the greatest contempt for such people as little nuns, there are times when "Discretion is the better part of valour." He hastily pulled up four turnips, tore off the leaves and folded them in his jacket. By this time an old nun had already come out.

"May Buddha preserve us, Ah Q! What made you climb into our garden to steal turnips! . . . Oh dear, what a wicked thing to do! Oh dear, Buddha preserve us! . . ."

"When did I ever climb into your garden and steal turnips?" retorted Ah Q, as he started off, still looking at her.

"Now — aren't you?" said the old nun, pointing at the folds of his jacket.

"Are these yours? Can you make them answer you? You. . . ."

Leaving his sentence unfinished, Ah Q took to his heels as fast as he could, followed by an enormously fat, black dog. Originally this dog had been at the front gate, and how it reached the back garden was a mystery. With a snarl the black dog gave chase and was just about to bite Ah Q's leg when most opportunely a turnip fell from his jacket, and the dog, taken by surprise, stopped for a second. During this time Ah Q scrambled up the mulberry tree, scaled the mud wall and fell, turnips and all, outside the convent. He left the black dog still barking by the mulberry tree, and the old nun saying her prayers.

Fearing that the nun would let the black dog out again, Ah Q gathered together his turnips and ran, picking up a few small stones as he went. But the black dog did not reappear. Ah Q threw away the stones and walked on, eating as he went, thinking to himself: "There is nothing to be had here; I had better go to town. . . ."

By the time he had finished the third turnip, he had made up his mind to go to town.

CHAPTER 6

From Restoration to Decline

WEICHUANG did not see Ah Q again till just after the Moon Festival that year. Everybody was surprised to hear of his return, and this made them think back and wonder where he had been all that time. The few previous occasions on which Ah Q had been to town, he had usually informed people in advance with great gusto; but since he had not done so this time, no one had noticed his going. He might have told the old man in charge of the Tutelary God's Temple, but according to the custom of Weichuang it was only when Mr. Chao, Mr. Chien, or the successful county candidate went to town that it was considered important. Even the Imitation Foreign Devil's going was not talked about, much less Ah Q's. This would explain why the old man had not spread the news for him, with the result that the villagers had had no means of knowing.

Ah Q's return this time was very different from before, and in fact quite enough to occasion astonishment. The day was growing dark when he appeared blinking sleepily before the door of the wineshop, walked up to the counter, pulled a handful of silver and coppers from his belt and tossed them on the counter. "Cash!" he said. "Bring the wine!" He was wearing a new, lined jacket, and at his waist evidently hung a large purse, the great weight of which caused his belt to sag in a sharp curve. It was the custom in Weichuang that when there seemed to be something unusual about anyone, he should be treated with respect rather than insolence, and now, although they knew quite well that this was Ah Q, still he was very different from the Ah Q of the ragged coat. The ancients say, "A scholar who has been away three days must be looked at with new eyes." So the waiter, innkeeper, customers and passers-by, all quite naturally expressed a kind of suspicion mingled with respect. The innkeeper started by nodding, then said:

"Hullo, Ah Q, so you're back!"

"Yes, I'm back."

"You've made money . . . er . . . where . . . ?"

"I went to town."

By the next day this piece of news had spread through Weichuang. And since everybody wanted to hear the success story of this Ah Q of the ready money and the new lined jacket, in the wineshop, tea-house, and under the temple eaves, the villagers gradually ferreted out the news. The result was that they began to treat Ah Q with a new deference.

According to Ah Q, he had been a servant in the house of a successful provincial candidate. This part of the story filled all who heard it with awe. This successful provincial candidate was named Pai, but because he was the only successful provincial candidate in the whole town there was no need to use his surname: whenever anyone spoke of the successful provincial candidate, it meant him. And this was so not only in Weichuang but everywhere within a radius of thirty miles, as if everybody imagined his name to be Mr. Successful Provincial Candidate. To have worked in the household of such a man naturally called for respect; but according to Ah Q's further statements, he was unwilling to go on working there because this successful candidate was really too much of a "turtle's egg." This part of the story made all who heard it sigh, but with a sense of pleasure, because it showed that Ah Q was actually not fit to work in such a man's household, yet not to work was a pity.

According to Ah Q, his return was also due to the fact that he was not satisfied with the townspeople because they called a long bench a straight bench, used shredded shallots to fry fish, and — a defect he had recently discovered — the women did not sway in a very satisfactory manner as they walked. However, the town had its good points too; for instance, in Weichuang everyone played with thirty-two bamboo counters, and only the Imitation Foreign Devil could play mah-jong, but in town even the street urchins excelled at mah-jong. You had only to place the Imitation Foreign Devil in the hands of these young rascals in their teens, for him straightway to become like "a small devil before the King of Hell." This part of the story made all who heard it blush.

"Have you seen an execution?" asked Ah Q. "Ah, that's a fine sight. . . . When they execute the revolutionaries. . . . Ah, that's a fine sight, a fine sight. . . ." As he shook his head, his spittle flew on to the face of Chao Szu-chen who stood directly opposite. This part of the story made all who heard it tremble. Then with a glance around, he suddenly raised his right hand and dropped it on the neck of Whiskers Wang, who, his head thrust forward, was listening with rapt attention.

"Kill!" shouted Ah Q.

Whiskers Wang gave a start, and drew in his head as fast as lightning or a spark struck from a flint, while the bystanders shivered with pleasurable apprehension. After this, Whiskers Wang went about in a daze for many days, and dared not go near Ah Q, nor did the others.

Although we cannot say that in the eyes of the inhabitants of Weichuang Ah Q's status at this time was superior to that of Mr. Chao, we can at least affirm without any danger of inaccuracy that it was about the same.

Not long after, Ah Q's fame suddenly spread into the women's apartments of Weichuang too. Although the only two families of any pretensions in Weichuang were those of Chien and Chao, and nine-tenths of the rest were poor, still women's apartments are women's apartments, and the way Ah Q's fame spread into them was something of a miracle. When the womenfolk met they would say to each other, "Mrs. Tsou bought a blue silk skirt from Ah Q. Although it was old, it only cost ninety cents. And Chao Pai-yen's mother (this has yet to be verified, because some say it was Chao Szu-chen's mother) bought a child's costume of crimson foreign calico, which was nearly new, for only three hundred cash, less eight per cent discount."

Then those who had no silk skirt or needed foreign calico were most anxious to see Ah Q in order to buy from him. Far from avoiding him now, they sometimes followed him when he passed, calling to him to stop.

"Ah Q, have you any more silk skirts?" they would ask. "No? We want foreign calico too. Do you have any?"

This news later spread from the poor households to the rich ones, because Mrs. Tsou was so pleased with her silk skirt that she took it to Mrs. Chao for her approval, and Mrs. Chao told Mr. Chao, speaking very highly of it.

Mr. Chao discussed the matter that evening at dinner with his son, the successful county candidate, suggesting that there must be something queer about Ah Q, and that they should be more careful about their doors and windows. They did not know, though, whether Ah Q had any things left or not, and thought he might still have something good. Since Mrs. Chao happened to want a good, cheap, fur jacket, after a family council it was decided to ask Mrs. Tsou to find Ah Q for them at once. For this a third exception was made to the rule, special permission being given that evening for a lamp to be lit.

A considerable amount of oil had been burned, but still there was no sign of Ah Q. The whole Chao household was yawning with impatience, some of them resented Ah Q's undisciplined ways, others angrily blamed Mrs. Tsou for not trying harder to get him there. Mrs. Chao was afraid that Ah Q dared not come because of the terms agreed upon that spring, but Mr. Chao did not think this anything to worry about, because, as he said, "This time *I* sent for him." Sure enough, Mr. Chao proved himself a man of insight, for Ah Q finally arrived with Mrs. Tsou.

"He keeps saying he has nothing left," panted Mrs. Tsou as she came in. "When I told him to come and tell you so himself he went on talking. I told him. . . ."

"Sir!" said Ah Q with an attempt at a smile, coming to a halt under the eaves.

"I hear you got rich out there, Ah Q," said Mr. Chao, going up to him and looking him over carefully. "Very good. Now . . . they say you have some old things. . . . Bring them all here for us to look at. . . . This is simply because I happen to want. . . ."

"I told Mrs. Tsou — there is nothing left."

"Nothing left?" Mr. Chao could not help sounding disappointed. "How could they go so quickly?"

"They belonged to a friend, and there was not much to begin with. People bought some. . . ."

"There must be something left."

"There is only a door curtain left."

"Then bring the door curtain for us to see," said Mrs. Chao hurriedly.

"Well, it will be all right if you bring it tomorrow," said Mr. Chao without much enthusiasm. "When you have anything in future, Ah Q, you must bring it to us first. . . ."

"We certainly will not pay less than other people!" said the successful county candidate. His wife shot a hasty glance at Ah Q to see his reaction.

"I need a fur jacket," said Mrs. Chao.

Although Ah Q agreed, he slouched out so carelessly that they did not know whether he had taken their instructions to heart or not. This made Mr. Chao so disappointed, annoyed and worried that he even stopped yawning. The successful candidate was also far from satisfied with Ah Q's attitude, and said, "People should be on their guard against such a turtle's egg. It might be best to order the bailiff to forbid him to live in Weichuang."

Mr. Chao did not agree, saying that he might bear a grudge, and that in a business like this it was probably a case of "the eagle does not prey on its own nest": his own village need not worry, and they need only be a little more watchful at night. The successful candidate, much impressed by this parental instruction, immediately withdrew his proposal for driving Ah Q away, but cautioned Mrs. Tsou on no account to repeat what he had said.

The next day, however, when Mrs. Tsou took her blue skirt to be dyed black she repeated these insinuations about Ah Q, although not actually mentioning what the successful candidate had said about driving him away. Even so, it was most damaging to Ah Q. In the first place, the bailiff appeared at his door and took away the door curtain. Although Ah Q protested that Mrs. Chao wanted to see it, the bailiff would not give it back, and even demanded a monthly payment of hush-money. In the second place, the villagers' respect for him suddenly changed. Although they still dared not take liberties, they avoided him as much as possible. While this differed from their previous fear of his "Kill!", it closely resembled the attitude of the ancients to spirits: they kept a respectful distance.

Some idlers who wanted to get to the bottom of the business went to question Ah Q carefully. And with no attempt at concealment, Ah Q told them proudly of his experiences. They learned that he had merely been a petty thief, not only unable to climb walls, but even unable to go through openings: he simply stood outside an opening to receive the stolen goods.

One night he had just received a package and his chief had gone in again, when he heard a great uproar inside, and took to his heels as fast as he could. He fled from the town that same night, back to Weichuang; and after this he dared not return to such a business. This story, however, was even more damaging to Ah Q, since the villagers had been keeping a respectful distance because they did not want to incur his enmity; for who could have guessed that he was only a thief who dared not steal again? Now they knew he was really too low to inspire fear.

CHAPTER 7

The Revolution

ON the fourteenth day of the ninth moon of the third year in the reign of Emperor Hsuan Tung[1] — the day on which Ah Q sold his purse to Chao Pai-yen — at midnight, after the fourth stroke of the third watch, a large boat with a big black awning came to the Chao family's landing place. This boat floated up in the darkness while the villagers were sound asleep, so that they knew nothing about it; but it left again about dawn, when quite a number of people saw it. Investigation revealed that this boat actually belonged to the successful provincial candidate!

This incident caused great uneasiness in Weichuang, and before midday the hearts of all the villagers were beating faster. The Chao family kept very quiet about the errand of the boat, but according to the gossip in the tea-house and wineshop, the revolutionaries were going to enter the town and the successful provincial candidate had come to the country to take refuge. Mrs. Tsou alone thought otherwise, maintaining that the successful provincial candidate merely

---

[1] The day on which Shaohsing was freed in the 1911 Revolution.

wanted to deposit a few battered cases in Weichuang, but that Mr. Chao had sent them back. Actually the successful provincial candidate and the successful county candidate in the Chao family were not on good terms, so that it was scarcely logical to expect them to prove friends in adversity; moreover, since Mrs. Tsou was a neighbour of the Chao family and had a better idea of what was going on, she ought to have known.

Then a rumour spread to the effect that although the scholar had not arrived himself, he had sent a long letter tracing some distant relationship with the Chao family; and since Mr. Chao after thinking it over had decided it could, after all, do him no harm to keep the cases, they were now stowed under his wife's bed. As for the revolutionaries, some people said they had entered the town that night in white helmets and white armour — in mourning for Emperor Tsung Cheng.[1]

Ah Q had long since known of revolutionaries, and this year with his own eyes had seen revolutionaries being decapitated. But since it had occurred to him that the revolutionaries were rebels and that a rebellion would make things difficult for him, he had always detested and kept away from them. Who could have guessed they could so frighten a successful provincial candidate renowned for thirty miles around? In consequence, Ah Q could not help feeling rather "entranced," the terror of all the villagers only adding to his delight.

---

[1] Tsung Cheng, the last emperor of the Ming dynasty, reigned from 1628 to 1644. He hanged himself before the Manchus entered Peking.

"Revolution is not a bad thing," thought Ah Q. "Finish off the whole lot of them . . . curse them! . . . I would like to go over to the revolutionaries myself."

Ah Q had been hard up recently, and was probably rather dissatisfied; added to this, he had drunk two bowls of wine at noon on an empty stomach. Consequently, he became drunk very quickly; and as he walked along thinking to himself, he felt again as if he were treading on air. Suddenly, in some curious way, he felt as if the revolutionaries were himself, and all the people in Weichuang were his captives. Unable to contain himself for joy, he could not help shouting loudly:

"Rebellion! Rebellion!"

All the villagers looked at him in consternation. Ah Q had never seen such pitiful looks before, and found them as refreshing as a drink of iced water in midsummer. So he walked on even more happily, shouting:

"All right . . . I shall take what I want! I shall like whom I please!

> *"Tra la, tra la!*
> *"I regret to have killed by mistake my sworn*
> *   brother Cheng, in my cups.*
> *"I regret to have killed . . . yah, yah, yah!*
> *"Tra la, tra la, tum ti tum tum!*
> *"I'll thrash you with a steel mace."*

Mr. Chao and his son were standing at their gate with two relatives discussing the revolution. Ah Q did not see them as he passed with his head thrown back, singing, *"Tra la la, tum ti tum!"*

"Q, old chap!" called Mr. Chao timidly in a low voice.

"Tra la!" sang Ah Q, unable to imagine that his name could be linked with those words "old chap." Sure that he had heard wrongly and was in no way concerned, he simply went on singing, *"Tra la la, tum ti tum!"*

"Q, old chap!"

"I regret to have killed. . . ."

"Ah Q!" The successful candidate had to call his name.

Only then did Ah Q come to a stop. "Well?" he asked with his head on one side.

"Q, old chap . . . now. . . ." But Mr. Chao was at a loss for words again. "Are you getting rich now?"

"Getting rich? Of course. I take what I like. . . ."

"Ah — Q, old man, poor friends of yours like us can't possibly matter . . ." said Chao Pai-yen apprehensively, as if sounding out the revolutionaries' attitude.

"Poor friends? Surely you are richer than I am," replied Ah Q, and walked away.

They stood there despondent and speechless; then Mr. Chao and his son went back to the house, and that evening discussed the question until it was time to light the lamps. When Chao Pai-yen went home he took the purse from his waist and gave it to his wife to hide for him at the bottom of a chest.

For some time Ah Q seemed to be walking on air, but by the time he reached the Tutelary God's Temple he was sober again. That evening the old man in charge of the temple was also unexpectedly friendly and offered him tea. Then Ah Q asked him for two flat cakes, and after eating these demanded a four-ounce candle that had been used, and a candlestick. He lit the candle and lay down alone in his little room. He felt inexpressibly refreshed and happy, while the candlelight leaped and flickered as on the Lantern Festival and his imagination soared with it.

"Revolt? It would be fun. . . . A group of revolutionaries would come, all wearing white helmets and white armour, carrying swords, steel maces, bombs, foreign guns, double-edged knives with sharp points and spears with hooks. They would come to the Tutelary God's Temple and call out, 'Ah Q! Come with us, come with us!' And then I would go with them. . . .

"Then all those villagers would be in a laughable plight, kneeling down and pleading, 'Ah Q, spare our lives.' But who would listen to them! The first to die would be Young D and Mr. Chao, then the successful county candidate and the Imitation Foreign Devil . . . but perhaps I would spare a few. I would once have spared Whiskers Wang, but now I don't even want him. . . .

"Things . . . I would go straight in and open the cases: silver ingots, foreign coins, foreign calico jackets. . . . First I would move the Ningpo bed of the successful county candidate's wife to the temple, and also move in the Chien family tables and chairs — or else just use the Chao family's. I would not lift a finger myself, but order Young D to move the things for me, and to look smart about it, unless he wanted a slap in the face. . . .

"Chao Szu-chen's younger sister is very ugly. In a few years Mrs. Tsou's daughter might be worth considering. The Imitation Foreign Devil's wife is willing to sleep with a man without a pigtail, hah! She can't be a good woman! The successful county candidate's wife has scars on her eyelids. . . . I have not seen Amah Wu for a long time, and don't know where she is — what a pity her feet are so big."

48

Before Ah Q had reached a satisfactory conclusion, there was a sound of snoring. The four-ounce candle had burned down only half an inch, and its flickering red light lit up his open mouth.

"Ho, ho!" shouted Ah Q suddenly, raising his head and looking wildly around. But when he saw the four-ounce candle, he lay back and went to sleep again.

The next morning he got up very late, and when he went out into the street everything was the same as usual. He was still hungry, but though he racked his brains he did not seem able to think of anything. Suddenly an idea came to him, and he walked slowly off, until either by design or accident he reached the Convent of Quiet Self-improvement.

The convent was as peaceful as it had been that spring, with its white wall and shining black gate. After a moment's reflection, he knocked at the gate, whereupon a dog started barking within. He hastily picked up several pieces of broken brick, then went up again to knock more heavily, knocking until a number of small dents appeared on the black gate. At last he heard someone coming to open the door.

Holding his broken bricks, Ah Q hastily stood with his legs wide apart, prepared to do battle with the black dog. The convent door opened a crack, and no black dog rushed out. When he looked in all he could see was the old nun.

"What are you here for again?" she asked, giving a start.

"There is a revolution . . . don't you know?" said Ah Q vaguely.

"Revolution, revolution . . . there has already been one," said the old nun, her eyes red from crying. "What do you think will become of us with all your revolutions?"

"What?" asked Ah Q in astonishment.

"Didn't you know? The revolutionaries have already been here!"

"Who?" asked Ah Q in even greater astonishment.

"The successful county candidate and the Imitation Foreign Devil."

This came as a complete surprise to Ah Q, who could not help being taken aback. When the old nun saw that he had lost his aggressiveness, she quickly shut the gate, so that when Ah Q pushed it again he could not budge it, and when he knocked again there was no answer.

It had happened that morning. The successful county candidate in the Chao family learned the news quickly, and as soon as he heard that the revolutionaries had entered the town that night, he immediately wound his pigtail up on his head and went out first thing to call on the Imitation Foreign Devil in the Chien family, with whom he had never been on good terms before. Because this was a time for all to work for reforms, they had a very pleasant talk and on the spot became comrades who saw eye to eye and pledged themselves to become revolutionaries.

After racking their brains for some time, they remembered that in the Convent of Quiet Self-improvement there was an imperial tablet inscribed "Long Live the Emperor" which ought to be done away with at once. Thereupon they lost no time in going to the convent to carry out their revolutionary activities. Because the old nun tried to stop them, and put in a few words, they considered her as the Manchu government and knocked her on the head many times with a stick and with their knuckles. The nun, pulling herself together after they had gone, made an inspection.

Naturally the imperial tablet had been smashed into fragments on the ground, and the valuable Hsuan Te censer[1] before the shrine of Kuan-yin, the goddess of mercy, had also disappeared.

Ah Q only learned this later. He deeply regretted having been asleep at the time, and resented the fact that they had not come to call him. Then he said to himself, "Maybe they still don't know I have joined the revolutionaries."

---

[1] Highly decorative bronze censers were made during the Hsuan Te period (1426-1435) of the Ming dynasty.

CHAPTER 8

Barred from the Revolution

THE people of Weichuang became more reassured every day. From the news that was brought they knew that, although the revolutionaries had entered the town, their coming had not made a great deal of difference. The magistrate was still the highest official, it was only his title that had changed; and the successful provincial candidate also had some post — the Weichuang villagers could not remember these names clearly — some kind of official post; while the head of the military was still the same old captain. The only cause for alarm was that, the day after their arrival, some bad revolutionaries made trouble by cutting off people's pigtails. It was said that the boatman "Seven Pounder" from the next village had fallen into their clutches, and that he no longer looked presentable. Still, the danger of this was not great, because the Weichuang villagers seldom went to town to begin with, and those who had been considering a trip to town at once changed their minds in order to avoid this risk. Ah Q had been thinking of going to town to look up his old friends, but as soon as he heard the news he became resigned and gave up the idea.

It would be wrong, however, to say that there were no reforms in Weichuang. During the next few days the number of people who coiled their pigtails on their heads gradually increased, and, as has already been said, the first to do so was naturally the successful county candidate; the next were Chao Szu-chen and Chao Pai-yen, and after them Ah Q. If it had been summer it would not have been considered strange if everybody had coiled their pigtails on their heads or tied them in knots; but this was late autumn, so that this autumn observance of a summer practice on the part of those who coiled their pigtails could be considered nothing short of a heroic decision, and as far as Weichuang was concerned it could not be said to have had no connection with the reforms.

When Chao Szu-chen approached with the nape of his neck bare, people who saw him remarked, "Ah! Here comes a revolutionary!"

When Ah Q heard this he was greatly impressed. Although he had long since heard how the successful county candidate had coiled his pigtail on his head, it had never occurred to him to do the same. Only now when he saw that Chao Szu-chen had followed suit was he struck with the idea of doing the same himself. He made up his mind to copy them. He used a bamboo chopstick to twist his pigtail up on his head, and after some hesitation eventually summoned up the courage to go out.

As he walked along the street people looked at him, but nobody said anything. Ah Q was very displeased at first, then he became very resentful. Recently he had been losing his temper very easily. As a matter of fact his life

53

was no harder than before the revolution, people treated him politely, and the shops no longer demanded payment in cash, yet Ah Q still felt dissatisfied. He thought since a revolution had taken place, it should involve more than this. When he saw Young D, his anger boiled over.

Young D had also coiled his pigtail up on his head and, what was more, he had actually used a bamboo chopstick to do so too. Ah Q had never imagined that Young D would also have the courage to do this; he certainly could not tolerate such a thing! Who was Young D anyway? He was greatly tempted to seize him then and there, break his bamboo chopstick, let down his pigtail and slap his face several times into the bargain to punish him for forgetting his place and for his presumption in becoming a revolutionary. But in the end he let him off, simply fixing him with a furious glare, spitting, and exclaiming, "Pah!"

These last few days the only one to go to town was the Imitation Foreign Devil. The successful county candidate in the Chao family had thought of using the deposited cases as a pretext to call on the successful provincial candidate, but the danger that he might have his pigtail cut off had made him defer his visit. He had written an extremely formal letter, and asked the Imitation Foreign Devil to take it to town; he had also asked the latter to introduce him to the Liberty Party. When the Imitation Foreign Devil came back he asked the successful county candidate for four dollars, after which the successful county candidate wore a silver peach on his chest. All the Weichuang villagers were overawed, and said that this was the badge of the Persimmon Oil Party[1] equivalent to the rank of a Han Lin.[2]   As a result, Mr. Chao's prestige suddenly increased, far more so in fact than when his son first passed the official examination; consequently he started looking down on everyone else, and, when he saw Ah Q, tended to ignore him a little.

Ah Q was thoroughly discontented at finding himself continually ignored, but as soon as he heard of this silver peach he realized at once why he was left out in the cold. Simply to say that you had gone over was not enough to make anyone a revolutionary; nor was it enough merely to wind your pigtail up on your head; the most important thing was to get into touch with the revolutionary party.   In all his life he had known only two revolutionaries, one of whom had already lost his head in town, leaving only the Imitation Foreign Devil.   Unless he went at once to talk things over with the Imitation Foreign Devil, no way would be left open to him.

The front gate of the Chien house happened to be open, and Ah Q crept timidly in.   Once inside he gave a start, for there he saw the Imitation Foreign Devil standing in the middle of the courtyard dressed entirely in black, no doubt in foreign dress, and also wearing a silver peach.   In his hand he held the stick with which Ah Q was already acquainted to his cost, and the foot or so of hair which he had grown again fell over his shoulders, hanging dishevelled like Saint Liu's.[3]   Standing erect before him were Chao

---

[1] The Liberty Party was called *Tzu Yu Tang*. The villagers, not understanding the word Liberty, turned *Tzu Yu* into *Shih Yu*, which means persimmon oil.

[2] The highest literary degree in the Ching dynasty (1644-1911).

[3] An immortal in Chinese folk legend, portrayed with flowing hair.

Pai-yen and three others, all of them listening with the utmost deference to what the Imitation Foreign Devil was saying.

Ah Q tiptoed inside and stood behind Chao Pai-yen, wanting to utter a greeting, but not knowing what to say. Obviously he could not call the man "Imitation Foreign Devil," and neither "Foreigner" nor "Revolutionary" seemed suitable. Perhaps the best form of address would be "Mr. Foreigner."

But Mr. Foreigner had not seen him, because with eyes raised he was saying with great animation:

"I am so impulsive that when we met I kept saying, 'Old Hung, we should get on with it!' But he always answered 'Nein!' — that's a foreign word which you wouldn't understand. Otherwise we should have succeeded long ago. This is an instance of how cautious he is. He asked me again and again to go to Hupeh, but I wouldn't agree. Who wants to work in a small district town? . . ."

"Er — er —" Ah Q waited for him to pause, and then screwed up his courage to speak. But for some reason or other he still did not call him Mr. Foreigner.

The four men who had been listening gave a start and turned to stare at Ah Q. Mr. Foreigner too caught sight of him for the first time.

"What?"

"I. . . ."

"Clear out!" .

"I want to join. . . ."

"Get out!" said Mr. Foreigner, lifting the "mourner's stick."

Then Chao Pai-yen and the others shouted, "Mr. Chien tells you to get out, don't you hear!"

Ah Q put up his hands to protect his head, and without knowing what he was doing fled through the gate; but this time Mr. Foreigner did not give chase. After running more than sixty steps Ah Q slowed down, and began to feel most upset, because if Mr. Foreigner would not allow him to be a revolutionary, there was no other way open to him. In future he could never hope to have men in white helmets and white armour come to call him. All his ambition, aims, hope and future had been blasted at one stroke. The fact that people might spread the news and make him a laughing-stock for the likes of Young D and Whiskers Wang was only a secondary consideration.

Never before had he felt so flat. Even coiling his pigtail on his head now struck him as pointless and ridiculous. As a form of revenge he was very tempted to let his pigtail down at once, but he did not do so. He wandered about till evening, when after drinking two bowls of wine on credit he began to feel in better spirits, and in his mind's eye saw fragmentary visions of white helmets and white armour once more.

One day he loafed about until late at night. Only when the wineshop was about to close did he start to stroll back to the Tutelary God's Temple.

"Bang — bump!"

He suddenly heard an unusual sound, which could not have been firecrackers. Ah Q, who always liked excitement and enjoyed poking his nose into other people's business, went looking for the noise in the darkness. He thought he heard footsteps ahead, and was listening carefully when a

57

man suddenly rushed out in front of him. As soon as Ah Q saw him, he turned and followed as fast as he could. When that man turned, Ah Q turned too, and when after turning a corner that man stopped, Ah Q stopped too. He saw there was no one behind, and that the man was Young D.

"What is the matter?" asked Ah Q resentfully.

"Chao . . . the Chao family has been robbed," panted Young D.

Ah Q's heart went pit-a-pat. After telling him this, Young D left. Ah Q ran on, then stopped two or three times. However, since he had once been in the business himself, he felt exceptionally courageous. Emerging from the street corner, he listened carefully and thought he heard shouting; he also looked carefully and thought he could see a lot of men in white helmets and white armour, carrying off cases, carrying off furniture, even carrying off the Ningpo bed of the successful county candidate's wife; he could not, however, see them very clearly. He wanted to go nearer, but his feet were rooted to the ground.

There was no moon that night, and Weichuang was very still in the pitch darkness, as quiet as in the peaceful days of the ancient Emperor Fu Hsi.[1] Ah Q stood there until he lost interest, yet everything still seemed the same as before; in the distance people moved to and fro, carrying things, carrying off cases, carrying off furniture, carrying off the Ningpo bed of the successful county candidate's wife . . . carrying until he could hardly believe his own eyes. But he decided not to go nearer, and went back to the temple.

---

[1] One of the earliest legendary monarchs in China.

It was even darker in the Tutelary God's Temple. When he had closed the big gate he groped his way into his room, and only after he had been lying down for some time did he feel calm enough to begin thinking how this affected him. The men in white helmets and white armour had evidently arrived, but they had not come to call him; they had taken away many things, but there was no share for him — this was all the fault of the Imitation Foreign Devil, who had barred him from the rebellion. Otherwise how could he have failed to have a share this time?

The more Ah Q thought of it the angrier he grew, until he was in a towering rage. "So no rebellion for me, only for you, eh?" he exclaimed, nodding maliciously. "Curse you, you Imitation Foreign Devil — all right, be a rebel! A rebel is punished by having his head chopped off. I'll turn informer, and see you carried into town to have your head cut off — you and all your family. . . . Kill, kill!"

CHAPTER 9

The Grand Finale

AFTER the Chao family was robbed most of the people in Weichuang felt pleased yet fearful, and Ah Q was no exception. But four days later Ah Q was suddenly dragged into town in the middle of the night. It happened to be a dark night. A squad of soldiers, a squad of militia, a squad of police and five secret servicemen made their way quietly to Weichuang, and, after posting a machine-gun opposite the entrance, under cover of darkness they surrounded the Tutelary God's Temple. Ah Q did not rush out. For a long time nothing stirred in the temple. The captain grew impatient and offered a reward of twenty thousand cash. Only then did two militiamen summon up courage to jump over the wall and enter. With their co-operation from within, the others rushed in and dragged Ah Q out. But not until he had been carried out of the temple to somewhere near the machine-gun did he begin to sober up.

It was already midday by the time they reached town, and Ah Q found himself carried to a dilapidated yamen where, after taking five or six turnings, he was pushed into a small room. No sooner had he stumbled inside than the door, made of wooden bars to form a grating, closed upon his heels. The rest of the room consisted of three blank walls, and when he looked round carefully he saw two other men in a corner of the room.

Although Ah Q was feeling rather uneasy, he was by no means too depressed, because the room where he slept in the Tutelary God's Temple was in no way superior to this. The two other men also seemed to be villagers. They gradually fell into conversation with him, and one of them told him that the successful provincial candidate wanted to dun him for the rent owed by his grandfather; the other did not know why he was there. When they questioned Ah Q, he answered quite frankly, "Because I wanted to revolt."

That afternoon he was dragged out through the barred door and taken to a big hall, at the far end of which sat an old man with a cleanly shaven head. Ah Q took him for a monk at first, but when he saw soldiers standing guard and a dozen men in long coats on both sides, some with their heads clean-shaven like this old man and some with a foot or so of hair hanging over their shoulders like the Imitation Foreign Devil, all glaring furiously at him with grim faces, he knew this man must be someone important. At once the joints of his knees relaxed of their own accord, and he sank down.

"Stand up to speak! Don't kneel!" shouted all the men in the long coats.

Although Ah Q understood, he felt incapable of standing up: his body had involuntarily dropped to a squatting position, and improving on it he finally knelt down.

"Slave! . . ." exclaimed the long-coated men contemptuously. They did not insist on his getting up, however.

"Tell the truth and you will receive a lighter sentence," said the old man with the shaven head, in a low but clear voice, fixing his eyes on Ah Q. "I know everything already. When you have confessed, I will let you go."

"Confess!" repeated the long-coated men loudly.

"The fact is I wanted . . . to come . . ." muttered Ah Q disjointedly, after a moment's confused thinking.

"In that case, why didn't you come?" asked the old man gently.

"The Imitation Foreign Devil wouldn't let me!"

"Nonsense! It is too late to talk now. Where are your accomplices?"

"What? . . ."

"The people who robbed the Chao family that night."

"They didn't come to call me. They moved the things away themselves." Mention of this made Ah Q indignant.

"Where did they go? When you have told me I will let you go," repeated the old man even more gently.

"I don't know . . . they didn't come to call me. . . ."

Then, at a sign from the old man, Ah Q was dragged back through the barred door. The following morning he was dragged out once more.

Everything was unchanged in the big hall. The old man with the clean-shaven head was still sitting there, and Ah Q knelt down again as before.

"Have you anything else to say?" asked the old man gently.

Ah Q thought, and decided there was nothing to say, so he answered, "Nothing."

Then a man in a long coat brought a sheet of paper and held a brush in front of Ah Q, which he wanted to thrust into his hand. Ah Q was now nearly frightened out of his wits, because this was the first time in his life that his hand had ever come into contact with a writing brush. He was just wondering how to hold it when the man pointed out a place on the paper, and told him to sign his name.

"I — I — can't write," said Ah Q, shamefaced, nervously holding the brush.

"In that case, to make it easy for you, draw a circle!"

Ah Q tried to draw a circle, but the hand with which he grasped the brush trembled, so the man spread the paper on the ground for him. Ah Q bent down and, as painstakingly as if his life depended on it, drew a circle. Afraid people would laugh at him, he determined to make the circle round; however, not only was that wretched brush very heavy, but it would not do his bidding. Instead it wobbled from side to side; and just as the line was about to close it swerved out again, making a shape like a melon seed.

While Ah Q was ashamed because he had not been able to draw a round circle, the man had already taken back the paper and brush without any comment. A number of people then dragged him back for the third time through the barred door.

This time he did not feel particularly irritated. He supposed that in this world it was the fate of everybody at some time to be dragged in and out of prison, and to have to draw circles on paper; it was only because his circle had not been round that he felt there was a stain on his reputation. Presently, however, he regained composure by thinking, "Only idiots can make perfect circles." And with this thought he fell asleep.

That night, however, the successful provincial candidate was unable to go to sleep, because he had quarrelled with the captain. The successful provincial candidate had insisted that the most important thing was to recover the stolen goods, while the captain said the most important thing was to make a public example. Recently the captain had come to treat the successful provincial candidate quite disdainfully. So, banging his fist on the table, he said, "Punish one to awe one hundred! See now, I have been a member of the revolutionary party for less than twenty days, but there have been a dozen cases of robbery, none of them solved yet; and think how badly that reflects on me. Now this one has been solved, you come and argue like a pedant. It won't do! This is my affair."

The successful provincial candidate was very upset, but he still persisted, saying that if the stolen goods were not recovered, he would resign immediately from his post as assistant civil administrator. "As you please!" said the captain.

In consequence the successful provincial candidate did not sleep that night, but happily he did not hand in his resignation the next day after all.

The third time that Ah Q was dragged out of the barred door, was the morning following the night on which the successful provincial candidate had been unable to sleep. When he reached the big hall, the old man with the clean-shaven head was still sitting there as usual, and Ah Q also knelt down as usual.

Very gently the old man questioned him: "Have you anything more to say?"

Ah Q thought, and decided there was nothing to say, so he answered, "Nothing."

A number of men in long coats and short jackets put a white vest of foreign cloth on him. It had some black characters on it. Ah Q felt considerably disconcerted, because this was very like mourning dress, and to wear mourning was unlucky. At the same time his hands were bound behind his back, and he was dragged out of the yamen.

Ah Q was lifted on to an uncovered cart, and several men in short jackets sat down with him. The cart started off at once. In front were a number of soldiers and militiamen shouldering foreign rifles, and on both sides were crowds of gaping spectators, while what was behind Ah Q could not see. Suddenly it occurred to him — "Can I be going to have my head cut off?" Panic seized him and everything turned dark before his eyes, while there was a humming in his ears as if he had fainted. But he did not really faint. Although he felt frightened some of the time, the rest of the time he was quite calm. It seemed to him that in this world probably it was the fate of everybody at some time to have his head cut off.

He still recognized the road and felt rather surprised: why were they not going to the execution ground? He did not know that he was being paraded round the streets as a public example. But if he had known, it would have been the same; he would only have thought that in this world probably it was the fate of everybody at some time to be made a public example of.

Then he realized that they were making a detour to the execution ground, so, after all, he must be going to have his head cut off. He looked round him regretfully at the people swarming after him like ants, and unexpectedly in the crowd of people by the road he caught sight of Amah Wu. So that was why he had not seen her for so long: she was working in town.

Ah Q suddenly became ashamed of his lack of spirit, because he had not sung any lines from an opera. His thoughts revolved like a whirlwind: *The Young Widow at Her Husband's Grave* was not heroic enough. The words of "I regret to have killed" in *The Battle of Dragon and Tiger* were too poor. *I'll thrash you with a steel mace* was still the best. But when he wanted to raise his hands, he remembered that they were bound together; so he did not sing *I'll thrash you* either.

"In twenty years I shall be another. . . ."[1] In his agitation Ah Q uttered half a saying which he had picked up himself but never used before. The crowd's roar "Good!!!" sounded like the growl of a wolf.

The cart moved steadily forward. During the shouting Ah Q's eyes turned in search of Amah Wu, but she did not seem to have seen him for she was looking intently at the foreign rifles carried by the soldiers.

So Ah Q took another look at the shouting crowd.

At that instant his thoughts revolved again like a whirlwind. Four years before, at the foot of the mountain, he had met a hungry wolf which had followed him at a set distance, wanting to eat him. He had nearly died of fright, but luckily he happened to have an axe in his hand, which gave him the courage to get back to Weichuang. He had never forgotten that wolf's eyes, fierce yet cowardly, gleaming like two will-o'-the-wisps, as if boring into him from a distance. Now he saw eyes more terrible even than the wolf's: dull yet penetrating eyes that, having devoured his words, still seemed

---

[1] "In twenty years I shall be another stout young fellow" was a phrase often used by criminals before execution, to show their scorn of death. Believing in the transmigration of the soul, they thought that after death their souls would enter other living bodies.

eager to devour something beyond his flesh and blood. And these eyes kept following him at a set distance.

These eyes seemed to have merged into one, biting into his soul.

"Help, help!"

But Ah Q never uttered these words. All had turned black before his eyes, there was a buzzing in his ears, and he felt as if his whole body were being scattered like so much light dust.

As for the after-effects of the robbery, the most affected was the successful provincial candidate, because the stolen goods were never recovered. All his family lamented bitterly. Next came the Chao household; for when the successful county candidate went into town to report the robbery, not only did he have his pigtail cut off by bad revolutionaries, but he had to pay a reward of twenty thousand cash into the bargain; so all the Chao family lamented bitterly too. From that day forward they gradually assumed the air of the survivors of a fallen dynasty.

As for any discussion of the event, no question was raised in Weichuang. Naturally all agreed that Ah Q had been a bad man, the proof being that he had been shot; for if he had not been bad, how could he have been shot? But the consensus of opinion in town was unfavourable. Most people were dissatisfied, because a shooting was not such a fine spectacle as a decapitation; and what a ridiculous culprit he had been too, to pass through so many streets without singing a single line from an opera. They had followed him for nothing.

December 1921

ABOUT THE AUTHOR

LU HSUN, pseudonym of Chou Shu-jen, is the father of modern Chinese literature, and the greatest standard-bearer of the Chinese cultural revolution. He was born in Shaohsing, Chekiang Province, in 1881 and died in Shanghai in 1936. As early as 1918, the year before the May Fourth Movement, he published his story *A Madman's Diary*, calling on the Chinese people to rise and give battle to feudalism. Thereafter Lu Hsun identified his work with the Chinese people's revolution for which he waged a relentless struggle until his death. In his later years (after 1927) he was closer than ever to the Chinese Communist Party, and became a fearless fighter and great thinker of the proletariat.

A prolific writer, he wrote three volumes of short stories: *Call to Arms, Wandering* and *Old Tales Retold,* and sixteen volumes of essays including *Hot Air* and *The Grave.* Among his translations are Fadeyev's *The Nineteen,* Gogol's *Dead Souls* and Panteleev's *The Watch.* Lu Hsun also wrote a brief history of Chinese fiction.